AGE OF DINOSAURS: TRICERATOPS

AGE OF DINOSAURS:

Triceratops

SARA GILBERT

CREATIVE EDUCATION

Published by Creative Education
P.O. Box 227, Mankato, Minnesota 56002
Creative Education is an imprint of The Creative Company
www.thecreativecompany.us

Design and production by Blue Design
Art direction by Rita Marshall
Printed by Corporate Graphics in the United States of America

Photographs by Alamy (Interfoto, Mary Evans Picture Library),
Bridgeman Art Library (O. Cenig, Peter Snowball), Corbis
(Bettmann, Jonathan Blair, Louie Psihoyos, Louie Psihoyos/
Science Faction, Paul A. Souders, Bill Varie), Dreamstime
(Peterpolak), Getty Images (Ron Burton, DEA Picture Library,
Dorling Kindersley, Jeff Swensen), iStockphoto (Christoph
Ermel), Library of Congress, Sarah Yakawonis/Blue Design

Library of Congress Cataloging-in-Publication Data
Gilbert, Sara.
Triceratops / by Sara Gilbert.
p. cm. — (Age of dinosaurs)
Summary: An introduction to the life and era of the horned,
herbivorous dinosaur known as Triceratops, starting with
the creature's 1888 discovery and ending with present-day
research topics.
Includes bibliographical references and index.
ISBN 978-1-58341-977-9
1. Triceratops—Juvenile literature. I. Title. II. Series.

QE862.065G55 2010
567.915'8—dc22   2009025537

CPSIA: 120109 PO1089

First Edition
9 8 7 6 5 4 3 2 1

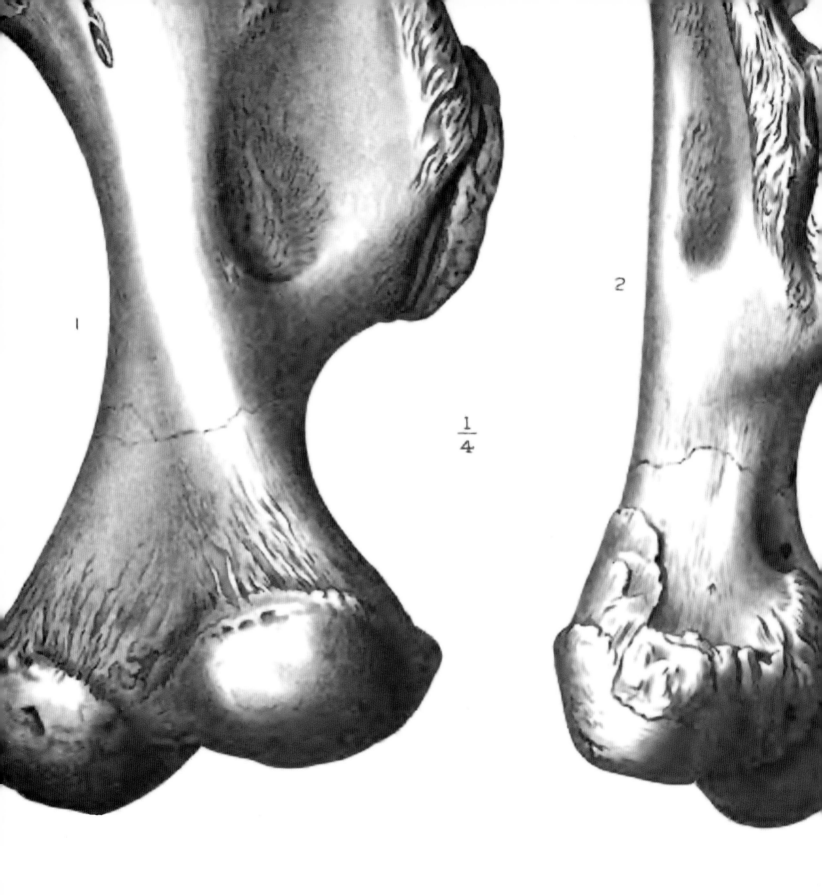

$\frac{1}{4}$

TRICERATOPS PRORSUS, Marsh

CONTENTS

TRICERATOPS TALES

HORNS AND A HEAD

John Bell Hatcher was on his way home. He had been sent out West by his boss, Othniel Charles (O. C.) Marsh, a renowned **paleontologist** and professor at Yale College who had hired him to hunt for fossils in the dry riverbeds of Wyoming. By the end of 1888, however, Hatcher had begun the long journey back to the East Coast. But then, as he was traveling through a canyon near Lusk, Wyoming, Hatcher saw a large fossilized **horn core** sticking out of the sandstone. He stopped to dig deeper and found that it was part of a giant skull buried deep in the rocks.

Even as the huge head was still more than half hidden, Hatcher sent word of his discovery to Marsh, who had received a pair of similar horns found near Denver, Colorado, a year earlier. Marsh had dismissed those horn cores as belonging to an early **species** of buffalo, but now he was intrigued; perhaps the horns were older than he had thought, and perhaps they belonged to a massive new dinosaur. He asked Hatcher to send the horn core to him—and then to keep digging.

When Marsh received the horn core from Hatcher, he compared it with those he had previously analyzed. It was, he discovered, from the same species. But on further inspection, he realized that the horns didn't belong to anything related to a buffalo. His suspicion was that Hatcher had happened upon a brand-new species of horned dinosaur that had existed during the Late Cretaceous Period (about 89 to 65

The massive size of *Triceratops* was appropriate for a creature that developed near the end of the dinosaur age, when many animals were getting progressively larger.

million years ago). Now the scientist eagerly awaited more news from his fossil hunter in Wyoming.

It was a monumental task for Hatcher to unearth the gigantic skull. Once it was free of the sandstone that had surrounded it for more than 65 million years, it had to be loaded onto a wagon and pulled by horses to the nearest railroad station. Then it was carefully placed in a train car and shipped back east.

During October and November of 1888, Hatcher shipped 71 boxes full of fossils, which weighed a collective 15,140 pounds (6,867 kg), back to Marsh at Yale's Peabody Museum. Included among those fossils was a gigantic skull that was almost 10 feet (3 m) long and weighed about half a ton (454 kg). It had a large frill, or a sheet of bone that extended backwards and up from its skull. The skull also featured three horn cores that were likely sheathed by dagger-like horns, the longest of which was almost three feet (0.9 m).

Although it was Hatcher who had found the skull, it was Marsh who studied it and, in 1889, named it *Triceratops*, which means "three-horned face." Other horned **herbivores** belonging to the Ceratopsidae family had already been unearthed, but this new species was far larger and more magnificent. The bones Hatcher had found represented only a portion of the entire skeleton, but it had clearly been an enormous dinosaur. Marsh could tell from the size of

Known as the "King of Collectors," John Bell Hatcher published almost 50 papers between 1893 and 1904 based on his extensive research.

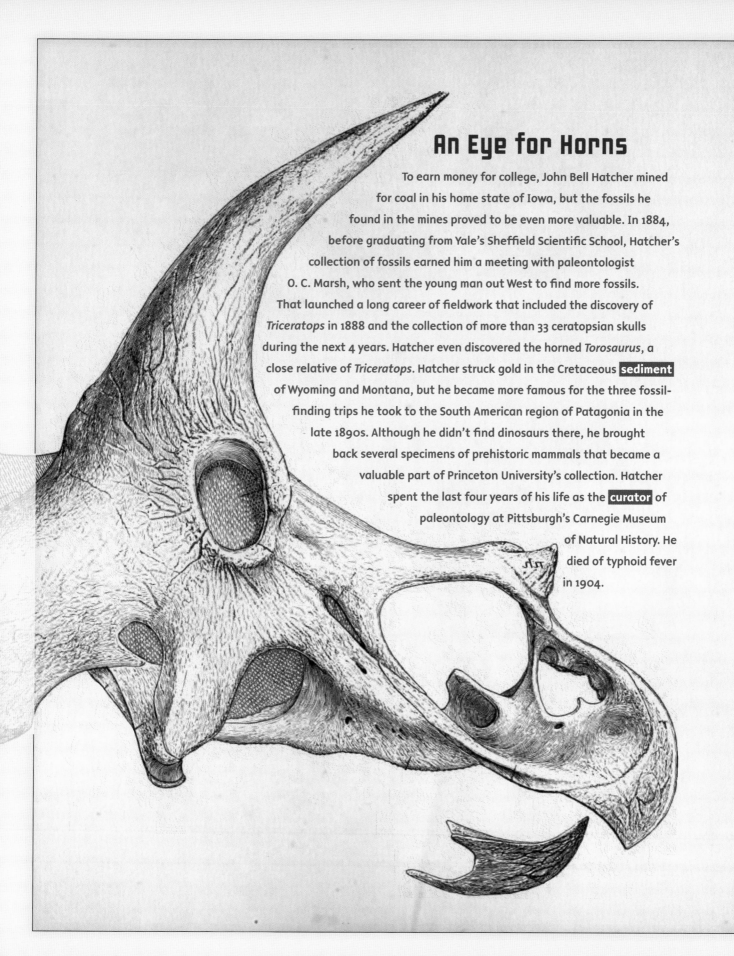

An Eye for Horns

To earn money for college, John Bell Hatcher mined for coal in his home state of Iowa, but the fossils he found in the mines proved to be even more valuable. In 1884, before graduating from Yale's Sheffield Scientific School, Hatcher's collection of fossils earned him a meeting with paleontologist O. C. Marsh, who sent the young man out West to find more fossils. That launched a long career of fieldwork that included the discovery of *Triceratops* in 1888 and the collection of more than 33 ceratopsian skulls during the next 4 years. Hatcher even discovered the horned *Torosaurus*, a close relative of *Triceratops*. Hatcher struck gold in the Cretaceous sediment of Wyoming and Montana, but he became more famous for the three fossil-finding trips he took to the South American region of Patagonia in the late 1890s. Although he didn't find dinosaurs there, he brought back several specimens of prehistoric mammals that became a valuable part of Princeton University's collection. Hatcher spent the last four years of his life as the curator of paleontology at Pittsburgh's Carnegie Museum of Natural History. He died of typhoid fever in 1904.

Naming Rights

In 1889, O. C. Marsh proudly named the new dinosaur species that his assistant John Bell Hatcher had found *Triceratops*—one of 80 dinosaurs that the well-known paleontologist named during his career. Marsh became famous for the number of dinosaurs he helped discover, but he gained just as much notoriety for the battle he waged with another prominent paleontologist—Edward Drinker Cope. Both men were so eager to name the most dinosaurs that they sometimes resorted to underhanded tactics. When one of them found a quarry filled with bones, the other would send a spy to check out what was being unearthed. They often vied for the same specimens at the same time and rushed to publish their findings about a particular species first, which frequently led to mistakes and inaccuracies. Although Marsh can honestly claim *Triceratops* as his own, a reptile that Cope found in Wyoming in 1872 and named *Agathaumas* has some striking similarities, especially in the drawings Cope did in his sketchbook. Some scientists wonder if Cope actually did find *Triceratops* first—but not enough evidence exists to change the record.

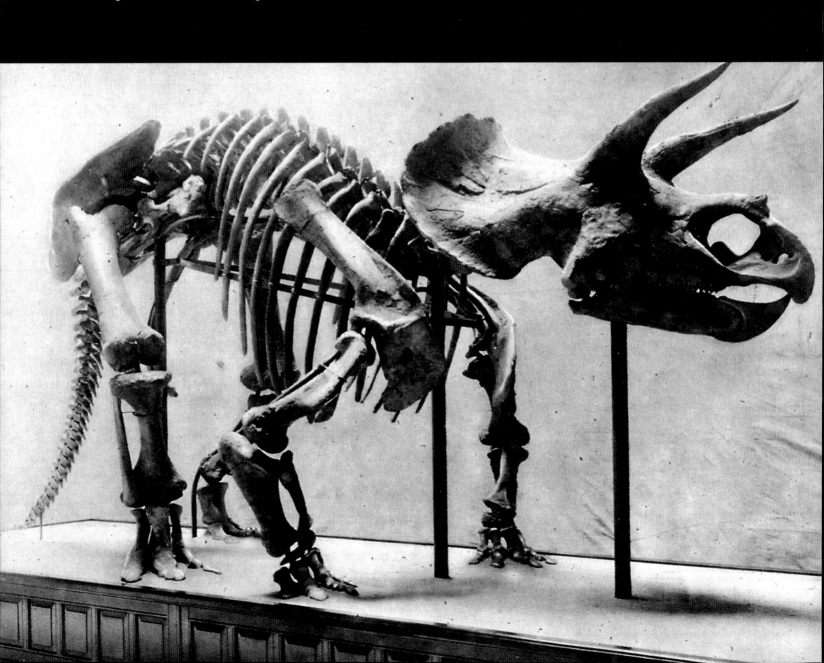

its head that it might have measured up to 30 feet (9 m) long and that it could have weighed several tons.

Naming it and unveiling its bones to the public was a crowning achievement for Marsh. At the time, he was engaged in an intense battle with another prominent paleontologist, Edward Drinker Cope, to name the most dinosaurs, and claiming *Triceratops* helped him pull even farther ahead of his rival. Marsh's excitement over *Triceratops* spilled over to the rest of the country and to many other parts of the world as well. The late 1800s had been a time of great dinosaur discoveries. Marsh had already named *Allosaurus*, *Apatosaurus*, and *Stegosaurus*, among dozens of others. The public had become increasingly fascinated by the gigantic creatures that paleontologists were unearthing, and Marsh reveled in being the center of so much attention.

In 1890, just a year after Marsh had dubbed the three-horned dinosaur *Triceratops*, the weekly English newspaper *Punch* printed a cartoon of Marsh presiding as the ringmaster over a circus of skeletons. He was dressed in an outfit emblazoned with stars and stripes and was standing on the back of an enormous *Triceratops* skull—the platform from which he directed the rest of his bony dinosaur performers.

Although such publicity brought Marsh the notoriety that he craved, it also fueled the interest of many other fossil hunters, each excited to find the next big dinosaur. Competition for dinosaur bones

Brachyceratops, another ceratopsid of the Late Cretaceous, is known primarily from juvenile specimens that have been found in Montana.

A Home for "Hatcher"

Washington, D.C.'s Smithsonian Institution was honored to unveil the first mounted *Triceratops* skeleton in the world in 1905—even if it had to piece it together from parts of more than 12 specimens. Some of those bones were even too small, as they had come from different dinosaur species. The feet, in fact, were from a duck-billed dinosaur. But the skeleton currently on display at the Smithsonian is much more authentic. In the early 1990s, museum staff realized that after almost a century on display, many of the dinosaur's bones were cracking. Experts dismantled the skeleton to repair it and preserve the bones. In the process, they modernized its stance and replaced the bones that didn't fit with better replicas. When they finished in 2001, they decided that the incredible dinosaur needed a name. The museum held a contest, asking children from around the country to submit an essay with their recommendation. The winning entry came from a 10-year-old boy named Jarek Buss, who lived in Laramie, Wyoming. He suggested that the dinosaur be named "Hatcher," in honor of the man who found the Smithsonian's original fossils in 1891.

Each horn above the eyes was about
3 feet (.9 m) long.

The lower jaw worked with the
beak to nip plants.

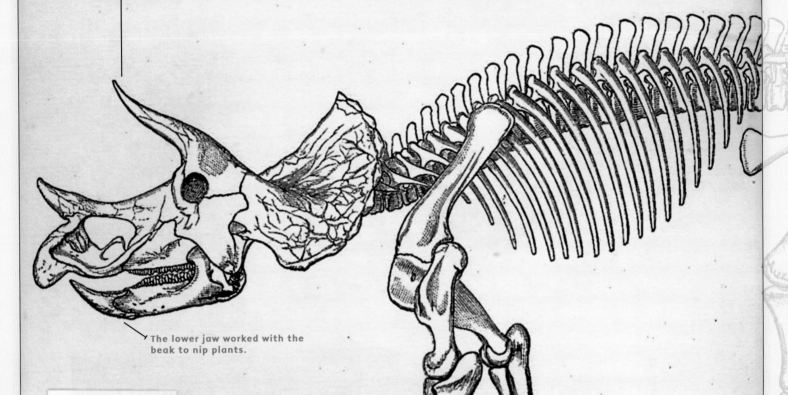

Best-known of the Ceratopsids

Triceratops

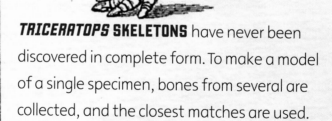

TRICERATOPS SKELETONS have never been
discovered in complete form. To make a model
of a single specimen, bones from several are
collected, and the closest matches are used.

N. 7705

increased over the next several years as more museums wanted to own them and more scientists became eager to study them.

Several more *Triceratops* fossils were found shortly after Hatcher's initial discovery. Hatcher himself unearthed 30 *Triceratops* skulls in Wyoming alone and found more than 40 other partial skeletons. In 1891, he dug up several *Triceratops* bones in Wyoming that were sold to the Smithsonian Institution in Washington, D.C. In 1905, those bones, combined with others that had been collected from several other *Triceratops* specimens, were reconstructed as the first mounted *Triceratops* anywhere in the world. That skeleton still stands at the Smithsonian today.

As hard as Hatcher looked, though, he was never able to find a complete *Triceratops* skeleton. No one else has, either. Dozens of partial specimens have been located throughout the western United States and Canada. The skulls have been remarkably well preserved, because they are so large and sturdy, and so many have been found that no one even knows the exact number. But much of what scientists do know today can be attributed to Hatcher's keen observational skills, as well as Marsh's careful study of the specimen found back in 1888.

The vertebral, or spinal, column of a *Triceratops* was lengthy, as the dinosaur had about 30 vertebrae along its back between the neck and tail.

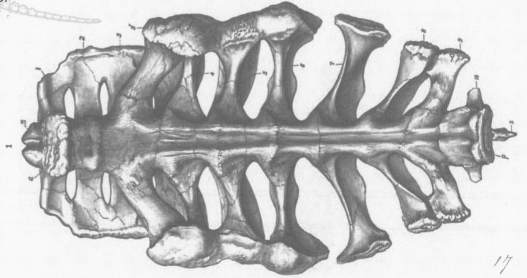

BIG AND BOUNTIFUL

Shrubs and ferns probably made up the majority of *Triceratops*'s leafy diet, and its beak-like mouth was perfectly designed to snap off vegetation.

There were dinosaurs that were bigger than the approximately 30-foot-long (9 m) and 5-ton (4.5 t) *Triceratops*. But during the Late Cretaceous Period, the 10-foot-tall (3 m) *Triceratops* and its horned ceratopsid relatives were among the most massive and numerous dinosaurs in North America.

As an herbivore, *Triceratops* was not designed with the quick feet, razor-sharp claws, or sawlike teeth of the predatory **carnivores**, including *Tyrannosaurus rex* (*T. rex*), that also roamed the forests of what is today western North America. But unlike the giant plant-eating sauropods of the Jurassic Period, which had long necks, long tails, and enormous girth, *Triceratops* was equipped with deadlier weapons.

The three horns on its head, which inspired its name, served as more than simply decoration. Each horn came to a sharp point at the tip. The two set up high, near its eyes, were quite long, each measuring perhaps three feet (0.9 m), or about the length of a golf club. The third, a nasal horn that jutted up just above its mouth, was much shorter—less than one foot (0.3 m) long.

Scientists believe that *Triceratops*'s horns were used as a **status symbol** to attract mates. Fossil evidence also suggests that both male and female *Triceratops* likely fought with each other, probably over mates or territory. Several skulls have been found marked with

Czech-born artist Zdenek Burian's illustrations of more than 500 books and shorter works became known for such active scenes of prehistoric life as this one of *T. rex* attacking and killing *Triceratops*.

deep gouges and scars where puncture wounds had healed in the dinosaur's cheeks and frills.

But scientists also believe that *Triceratops* occasionally used its horns to defend itself and its young from carnivores. Many would-be attackers were put off by the imposing horns, but *T. rex* was one of the few that would actively pursue a *Triceratops*. However, probably even that most fearsome of predators preyed only on those *Triceratops* that were weak, sick, or young. When a *T. rex* came too close to one of those vulnerable members, another protective *Triceratops* probably would have lowered its head and lifted its neck frill, trying to intimidate its enemy.

Terrifying *T. Rex*

Although *Triceratops* was a peaceful plant-eater, its huge head and long horns frightened many dinosaurs, including well-armed carnivores. But there was one predator that wasn't afraid to attack *Triceratops*: *Tyrannosaurus rex*. The gigantic predator was the most ferocious meat-eater of the Cretaceous Period. It measured between 40 and 45 feet (12–14 m) in length and weighed 5 to 7 tons (4.5–6.4 t). But what *Triceratops* feared most were the long, jagged teeth that lined the enormous jaws of *T. Rex*. Those teeth—at least 50 of them—were capable of not only tearing away an animal's flesh but also digging deeply into its bones. *T. rex* had to eat its own body weight in meat each week, which meant it was often on the prowl for prey. *Tyrannosaurus* probably preferred to catch dinosaurs that wouldn't put up a fight, taking advantage of young, weak, or injured *Triceratops*, or possibly even hunting in teams, with one *T. rex* distracting the victim and another lunging onto its unprotected side or back. Many *Triceratops* bones have been found that bear the telltale gouges of *T. rex* teeth.

The neck frill was a solid sheet of bone that was likely covered with skin, which in turn encased a network of blood vessels. Scientists have offered many theories about the frill's use, from helping *Triceratops* control its body temperature (by absorbing heat or cooling quickly) to providing an identifying color or pattern. They are fairly sure about one point: that the frill was used to frighten possible attackers. When the dinosaur felt threatened or angry, its frill might have reddened in color. That might have helped *Triceratops* appear bigger and tougher. If those intimidation tactics didn't work, *Triceratops* might have charged. Its horns would have inflicted serious injuries and possibly even killed some enemies.

*T*riceratops's skull was built for charging at predators or at each other. Like modern bighorn sheep, which smash into each other during annual mating rituals, *Triceratops* had extra space between the base of its brow horns and its brain. That space would have helped absorb the impact of crashing its head into another dinosaur, protecting its brain from injury.

The dinosaur's massive skull was also designed to enable *Triceratops* to graze contentedly on the lush vegetation covering the ground. *Triceratops* held its heavy head low to the ground and used its sharp beak—shaped much like a parrot's—

A distinctive skull, with its bony frill and horns, has made *Triceratops* one of the most recognizable and memorable dinosaurs for more than 100 years.

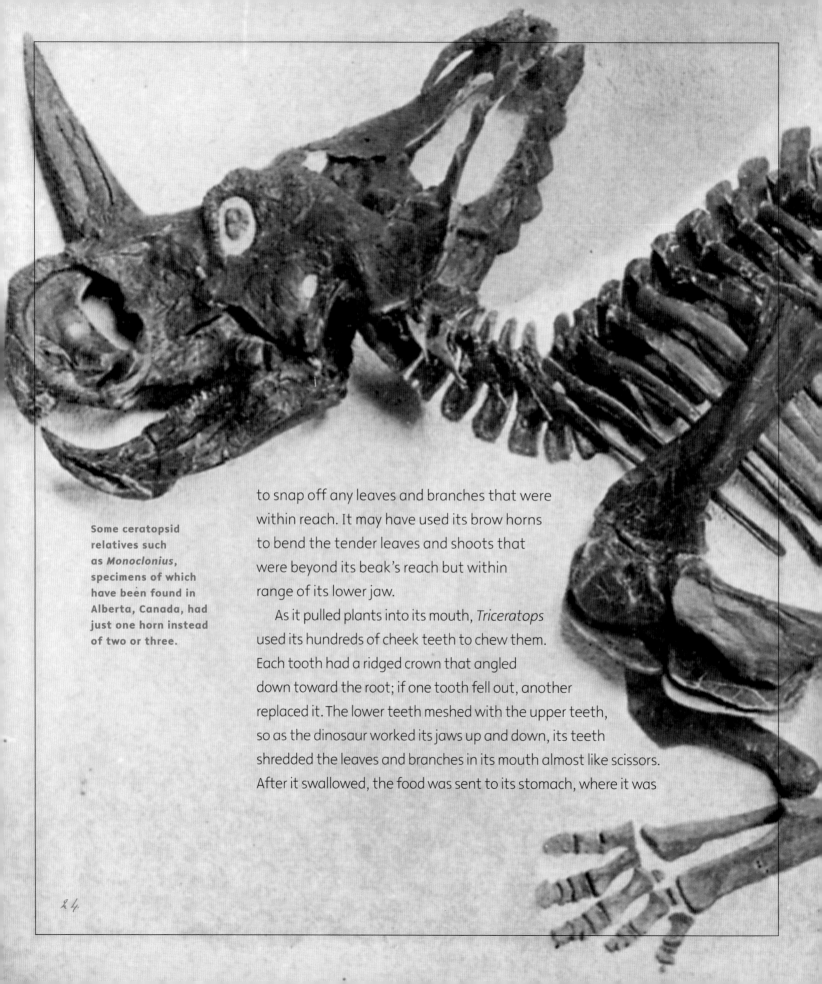

Some ceratopsid relatives such as *Monoclonius*, specimens of which have been found in Alberta, Canada, had just one horn instead of two or three.

to snap off any leaves and branches that were within reach. It may have used its brow horns to bend the tender leaves and shoots that were beyond its beak's reach but within range of its lower jaw.

As it pulled plants into its mouth, *Triceratops* used its hundreds of cheek teeth to chew them. Each tooth had a ridged crown that angled down toward the root; if one tooth fell out, another replaced it. The lower teeth meshed with the upper teeth, so as the dinosaur worked its jaws up and down, its teeth shredded the leaves and branches in its mouth almost like scissors. After it swallowed, the food was sent to its stomach, where it was ground up even more by several gastroliths, or smooth stones that the *Triceratops* had swallowed to help digest its food.

Each *Triceratops* had to eat enormous amounts of food daily to fuel its massive body. Large trackways, or trails of footprints fossilized in stone, suggest that the dinosaurs may have traveled in herds. Trackways of numerous footprints consistent with the width of *Triceratops* and other ceratopsian feet have been found in North and South America, which tells scientists that the dinosaurs may have **migrated** together as a group. Such a large group of *Triceratops* could have easily and quickly consumed all the available ground cover in an area. It's possible that *Triceratops* was constantly on the move, slowly plodding from one place to another and munching on any vegetation it could find.

Traveling in large numbers would have helped protect *Triceratops* from would-be predators. If a hungry carnivore approached, the full-grown dinosaurs likely would have formed a tight line or circle around the younger members of the herd, who probably traveled in the middle of the group. The adults probably stamped their feet and lowered their heads as signs of aggression. If necessary, one or two might have moved forward and attempted to chase the attacker away.

Although it generally moved quite slowly, scientists who have studied the pattern of footprints in *Triceratops* trackways believe that the animal was capable of surprising speed when the occasion called for it. If a *T. rex* was charging or threatening to attack, *Triceratops* could have probably run up to 25 miles (40 km) an hour. It was also capable of rearing up on its huge back legs to frighten an enemy or protect its young.

Most scientists believe that *Triceratops* babies were hatched from eggs that were laid in a nest. Those babies stayed close to their parents, probably relying on them for food until they were big enough to forage on their own. *Triceratops* mothers appeared to have stayed with their offspring and to have taken care of them. They seemed particularly protective of their young, who were vulnerable to attack from predators.

But *Triceratops* itself was a peaceful creature. It preferred to plod along and eat rather than to pick a fight with a predator. As long as there were fresh ferns and chewy **cycads** on which it could chomp, it was perfectly content to ramble through the forests.

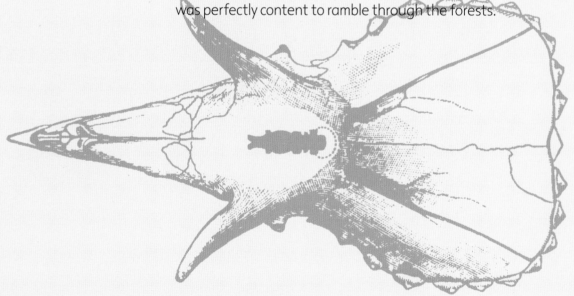

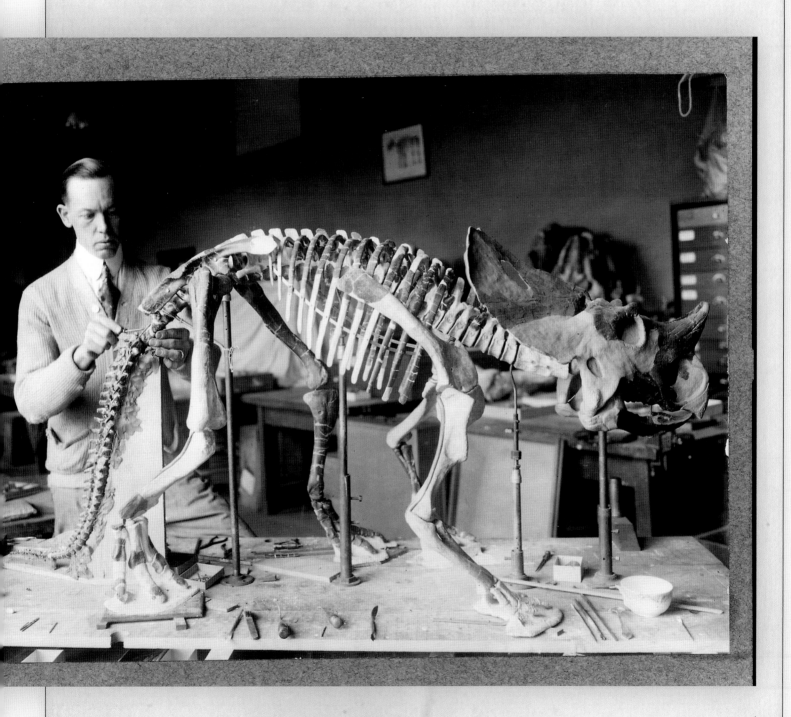

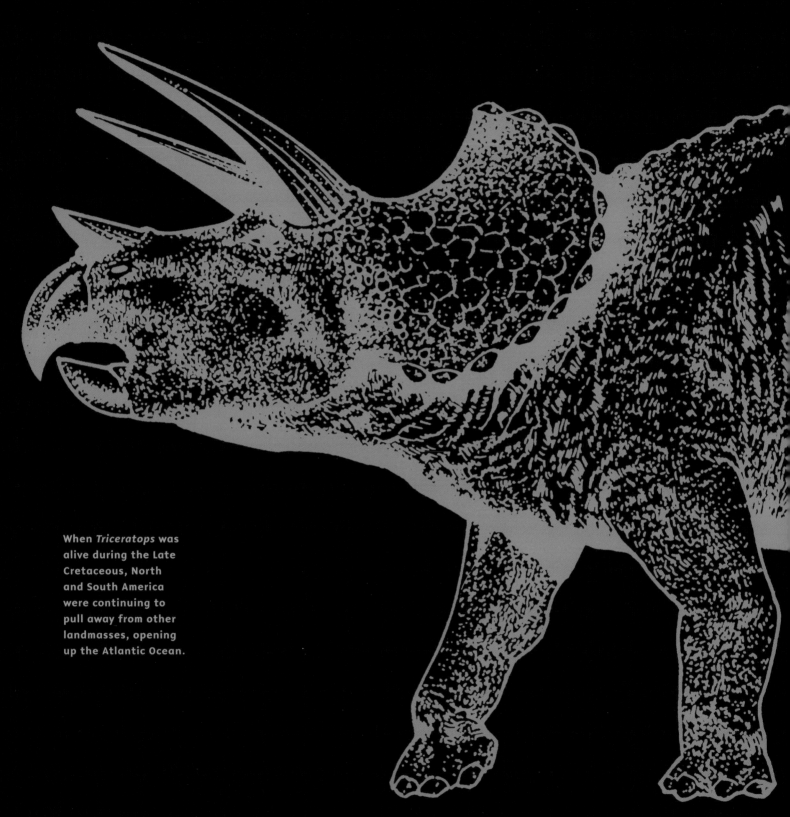

When *Triceratops* was alive during the Late Cretaceous, North and South America were continuing to pull away from other landmasses, opening up the Atlantic Ocean.

TIME FOR THE *TRICERATOPS*

*T*riceratops was one of the last dinosaurs to appear on Earth, **evolving** just a few million years before the end of the Cretaceous Period (which began approximately 144 million years ago) and the disappearance of all dinosaurs. By that time, between 68 and 65 million years ago, the earth was beginning to take on more of its current form.

Long ago, all of Earth's landmasses were connected as one supercontinent called Pangaea. During the period prior to the Cretaceous, the Jurassic, Pangaea broke into two major fragments that shifted to the northern and southern halves of the world— Laurasia was in the north, while Gondwana was in the south. Over millions of years, the seven continents that we know on Earth today broke away until they reached their current positions. This movement not only redrew the boundaries of the Atlantic and Pacific oceans, but it also caused collisions with pieces of the ocean floor. Several mountain ranges around the world—including the Rocky Mountains in what is now western North America—were formed in this way.

The shifting landmasses also brought about higher sea levels in some parts of the world and variations in **climates** throughout the globe. The overall climate grew warmer and wetter as the Jurassic Period progressed, and during the Cretaceous, the temperatures climbed to new heights. Tropical landscapes that are today found only in areas surrounding the equator were common throughout the world at that time.

As the temperature increased both on land and in the seas, marine creatures thrived in the deep, warm waters. Giant swimming lizards called mosasaurs were among the most feared predators. Sea turtles, on the other hand, presented a threat primarily to a species of small fish called teleosts. Most modern fish are descendants of these early teleosts, which developed the ability to swim faster, thanks to scales that had decreased in weight.

On land, small, colorful flowering plants began to appear, flourishing in the tropical environment. Landscapes were no longer dominated by the browns and greens of **conifers**, cycads, ferns, and **ginkgoes**. Although *Triceratops* enjoyed large meals made up of many of these options, it would have had more trouble reaching the leaves of the oak, maple, and walnut trees that were also beginning to grow in some parts of North America.

The environmental conditions of the Late Cretaceous favored explosive growth of both plants and creatures that would eat the new vegetation. *Triceratops* and horned relatives such as *Torosaurus* and *Monoclonius* joined the ornithischian, or bird-hipped, dinosaurs in enjoying the lush plant life that was widely available. Such herbivores had to develop sharper teeth in order to tear through the new flowering plants, and duck-bills such as *Edmontosaurus* foraged for food in herds that contained thousands of individuals. In fact, scientists note that the total number of dinosaur species on Earth increased

Torosaurus (below and opposite) had two holes in its frill that were probably covered by skin, unlike the solid-bone frill sported by Triceratops.

substantially sometime in the Late Cretaceous Period—perhaps by as much as 50 percent. Some scientists argue that such a percentage could be misleading, as the finding of more Late Cretaceous fossils does not necessarily signify that there were more dinosaurs alive at that time. They say that because fossils from that period are located closer to the earth's surface and are easier to find than many of those from earlier periods, it only makes it appear as though there were more species in existence during the Late Cretaceous.

Still, such profound growth in the number of plant-eaters was accompanied by the evolution of new predators as well. The most notorious of those hungry hunters was *T. rex*, one of the largest carnivores that ever lived and a confirmed predator of *Triceratops*. Smaller meat-eaters such as *Troodon* and *Albertosaurus* enjoyed a healthy diet of plant-eaters—but few of those predators would have risked attacking the massive and well-armed *Triceratops*. Another armored dinosaur species was *Ankylosaurus*, whose heavy tail club likely put off all but the most intent predators.

The generally peaceful, plodding *Triceratops* shared space on land with smaller **reptiles** as well as with **mammals**, which were evolving and diversifying rapidly. Snakes had appeared, as had early crocodiles, and mice, rats, and ancestors of modern opossums scampered through the underbrush. Flying reptiles called pterosaurs ruled the skies, but small birds were becoming more common and were developing their modern skeletal structures and feathers. The advent of flowering plants such as magnolias also brought about the first bees and other flying insects.

Scientists believe that there was a large body of water in the middle of the North American continent during the Cretaceous Period. Large trackways have been found on the western edge of where that sea was located. Some of the footprints in the trackways have been identified as belonging to *Triceratops* and other horned dinosaurs. Such evidence suggests that the creatures might have spent a great deal of time near the water, possibly because it would have provided fertile land for plants to grow.

*T*riceratops and its ceratopsid cousins were well suited to life on land during the Late Cretaceous. But no matter how well designed they were, they were not prepared to survive the disaster known as the K-T (Cretaceous-Tertiary) **extinction** event that wiped out not only every known species of dinosaur but also a great number of other animals

Ceratopsids were diverse, from the one-horned *Monoclonius* to *Styracosaurus*, which had four to six horns on its frill in addition to those on its face.

as well. Some scientists believe that up to 85 percent of the mammals, fish, and birds that existed then disappeared when the dinosaurs did.

Scientists have speculated for decades about what caused this mass extinction, and numerous theories have been offered. One possible cause involved the volcanoes that became increasingly active during the Cretaceous Period. Scientists know that at some point around the time of extinction, about 65 million years ago, there was a series of enormous volcanic eruptions on Earth. Clouds of dust and gases would have filled the sky, blocking the sun and resulting in a dramatic cooling effect that would have led to a mass extinction of the larger animals unable to withstand such temperatures.

The extinction event that wiped out the dinosaurs at the end of the Cretaceous ushered in the Tertiary Period, which is known as the age of mammals.

Most scientists, however, believe that *Triceratops* and the rest of the dinosaurs were destroyed by a major catastrophe caused by an impact from outer space. A meteor measuring approximately six miles (9.7 km) across is known to have struck the planet 65 million years ago near the coast of Mexico's Yucatán Peninsula. The impact likely resulted in a climate-changing scenario similar to the volcanic eruptions. Some scientists have even speculated that the dinosaurs—and other life on Earth—may have fallen victim to a combination of catastrophes around the same time. Although exactly what happened may never be known, the results are undeniable. By the time the Tertiary Period began, all of the dinosaurs on Earth—including *Triceratops*—had disappeared.

HUNTING FOR *TRICERATOPS*

*T*riceratops was one of the most abundant dinosaurs of the Late Cretaceous Period and has become the most famous and recognizable of all the horned dinosaurs. Scientists have been able to learn much about the species from the many bones that have been unearthed, including parts from at least 50 individual dinosaurs. But because no complete skeleton has yet been discovered, paleontologists have also had to dig for information about the hulking beast in different places.

Scientists have been able to learn about *Triceratops*'s migration habits and family groups by studying the trackways that have been fossilized in stone. They have also been able to learn about what the dinosaurs ate by analyzing the animal's coprolites, or fossilized droppings. The droppings of other contemporary dinosaurs have also

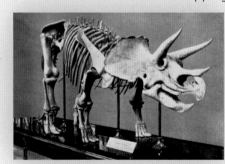

pointed to which predators were actually able to catch and kill *Triceratops*. Coprolites that appear to have been from a *T. rex*, for example, were found in Canada in 1995 and contained bone fragments that likely belonged to a *Triceratops*.

The study of its relatives has also helped scientists better understand *Triceratops*. Although each of the horned ceratopsids was unique, they shared many common features. Because they were so similar, scientists can make educated guesses about the family as a whole. New research has also helped clarify old assumptions that have been made about a dinosaur. When *Triceratops*

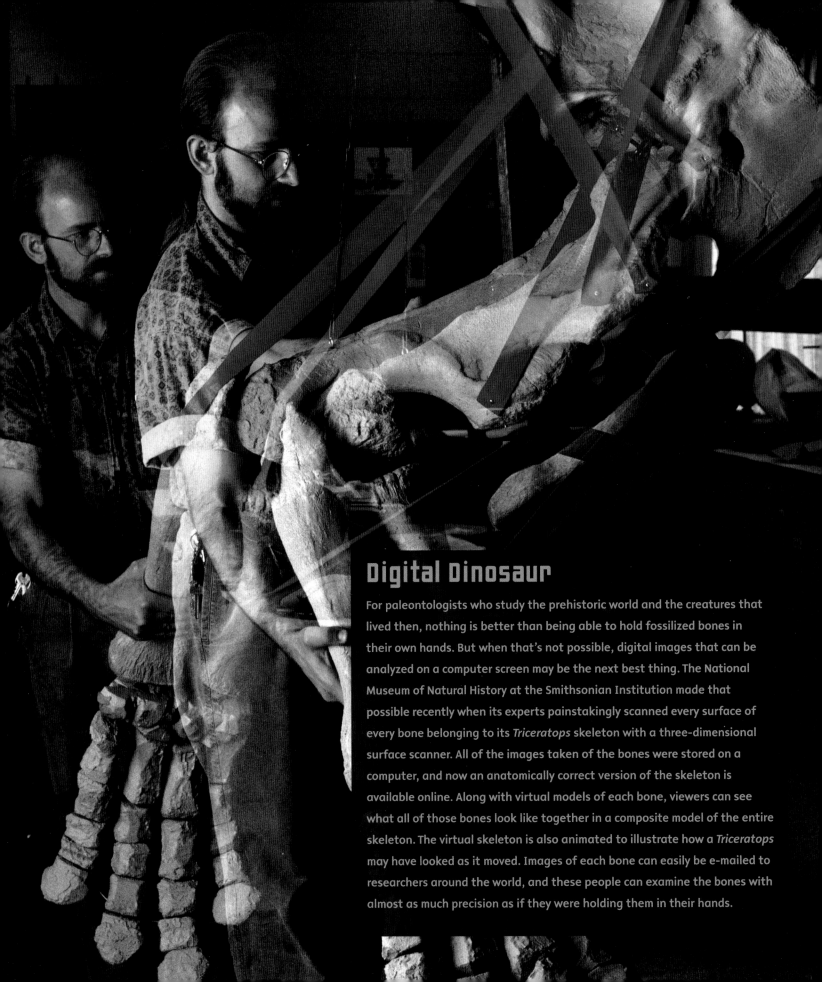

Digital Dinosaur

For paleontologists who study the prehistoric world and the creatures that lived then, nothing is better than being able to hold fossilized bones in their own hands. But when that's not possible, digital images that can be analyzed on a computer screen may be the next best thing. The National Museum of Natural History at the Smithsonian Institution made that possible recently when its experts painstakingly scanned every surface of every bone belonging to its *Triceratops* skeleton with a three-dimensional surface scanner. All of the images taken of the bones were stored on a computer, and now an anatomically correct version of the skeleton is available online. Along with virtual models of each bone, viewers can see what all of those bones look like together in a composite model of the entire skeleton. The virtual skeleton is also animated to illustrate how a *Triceratops* may have looked as it moved. Images of each bone can easily be e-mailed to researchers around the world, and these people can examine the bones with almost as much precision as if they were holding them in their hands.

was first discovered in the late 1800s, scientists thought that its body posture was similar to modern reptiles such as crocodiles. Early skeletal reconstructions showed the dinosaur with its four legs splayed out to its sides, instead of being positioned directly beneath its body.

By the 1980s, many scientists were beginning to believe that such reconstructions were not accurate. Some believed that animals the size of *Triceratops* would have had legs positioned more like the legs of a large modern mammal of similar weight—such as a rhinoceros. Others thought that it a might be a combination of the two. When the Smithsonian Institution dismantled its original *Triceratops* skeleton for preservation in the early 1990s, it used computer scans to analyze the position of the legs. Based on that research, the skeleton was put back together with its hind legs held straight underneath the body but its front legs slightly splayed to the sides.

In 1994, a rancher in North Dakota discovered a partial skeleton that added another dimension to the leg position controversy. Although the leg bones existed only on the right side of the specimen, they were fully articulated, or held together by joints. They were the first articulated *Triceratops* bones ever discovered, and they seemed to suggest that the dinosaur's stance was more like its contemporary ornithischian dinosaurs such as *Stegosaurus*. Experts are still considering what this discovery means and how it will influence their understanding of the dinosaur's posture.

Another remarkable *Triceratops* discovery was made in 1998, when a Wyoming couple found a portion of a skull peeking out of a hillside near their ranch. That complete skull led researchers to a skeleton

Along with virtual models, scientists also make physical replicas of dinosaur parts, using such materials as elastic bands to mimic muscles.

that is already known to be more than 50 percent complete. Scientists have been able to identify its ribs, **vertebrae**, femurs, and hipbones, all of which were remarkably preserved in a fossil bed from the Late Cretaceous. The skeleton, which has been named "Kelsey" in honor of the granddaughter of the couple who discovered it, may help resolve many mysteries about the dinosaur's bone structure.

John Bell Hatcher still holds the record for most *Triceratops* bones collected, but other paleontologists have had great success finding the ceratopsid's fossils as well. American paleontologist John Horner, who is best known for discovering parts of almost a dozen *Tyrannosaurus* skeletons during his career, also helped unearth the skull and frill of a baby *Triceratops* in Montana's Hell Creek region in the late 1990s. Only a few bones of young *Triceratops* have been found, and each one helps scientists better understand the dinosaur's life cycle. So far, though, no one has been able to offer an estimate of how long the animal lived.

Prehistoric creatures such as *Triceratops* have fascinated artists for the past century, especially with their possibilities for coloration.

Pictures of the Prehistoric

While paleontologists were busy reconstructing the skeletons of dozens of dinosaurs in the late 1800s, artist Charles R. Knight was busy fleshing out the prehistoric creatures with paint. Knight worked closely with American paleontologists Edward Drinker Cope and Henry Fairfield Osborn to bring the dinosaurs they discovered back to life—on canvas at least. Knight was known for his remarkable artwork—including a sculpture of a *Triceratops*—that portrayed dinosaurs in their natural environments. His drawings and illustrations were published in many books and magazines and helped create a picture of prehistoric life for average Americans in the early 1900s. Sometimes Knight's depictions also helped scientists at museums achieve more accurate reconstructions of skeletons. In 1901, Knight painted a picture of a *Triceratops* standing on an ancient hillside (which was erroneously covered with grass, a form of vegetation we now know could not have existed during *Triceratops*'s lifetime in the Cretaceous Period). The men charged with reconstructing the *Triceratops* bones that the Smithsonian Institution had purchased from bone hunter John Bell Hatcher in 1891 used Knight's painting as a model during the lengthy reconstruction process.

STORAGE

Disappearing Bones

Scientists have long been frustrated by the lack of complete *Triceratops* skeletons. Although they know that it was one of the most common animals in North America during the Late Cretaceous, they have encountered only bits and pieces of skeletons. Many *Triceratops* skulls have been found, but putting together the rest of their bodies for skeletal reconstructions requires pulling bones from several different specimens. While such a process is frustrating, scientists do understand why finding a complete skeleton has been such a challenge. When the great beasts died, **scavengers** would have hungrily pulled their bodies apart to get at the most meat. As they did that, many of the bones would have been broken or separated from the rest of the body. They may have been spread out across a wide area. Even dinosaur bones that stayed intact long after the dinosaur died would have probably been blown away by the wind or weathered into tiny pieces by rain and sunshine. Knowing how rare it is for skeletons to survive for millions of years makes it even more impressive when a specimen—complete or not—is discovered.

Horner, who is the chief curator of paleontology at the Museum of the Rockies in Bozeman, Montana, put that prized skull on display, along with the skulls of four other juvenile *Triceratops*. Other museums also possess skeletal reconstructions of *Triceratops*, including the Science Museum of Minnesota in St. Paul, Boston's Museum of Science, and the National Museum of Natural History at the Smithsonian Institution. Although none of these reconstructions has been compiled from the bones of one complete dinosaur, they are nonetheless impressive representations of the animal as a whole.

But neither professional paleontologists nor amateur fossil hunters have given up hope of finding an intact skeleton of the mighty herbivore someday. They remain on the lookout for any newly unearthed bones or fossils that might hold additional information about *Triceratops*'s existence and extinction. Despite the many technological advances that have come about in the years since Hatcher painstakingly dug out the first skull in 1888, removing and restoring dinosaur bones remains a time-consuming and labor-intensive process.

For many scientists, young and old, the work is worth the results. Any time they learn something new about *Triceratops* or another dinosaur, they come closer to understanding what life on Earth was like millions of years ago. More than 120 years after the first *Triceratops* bones were discovered, scientists are still learning more about them and their reptilian relatives. And a century from now, they will probably have still more to discover.

Other dinosaur skulls, such as that of *Tyrannosaurus rex* (opposite), are not often found as undamaged and complete as a *Triceratops*'s skull.

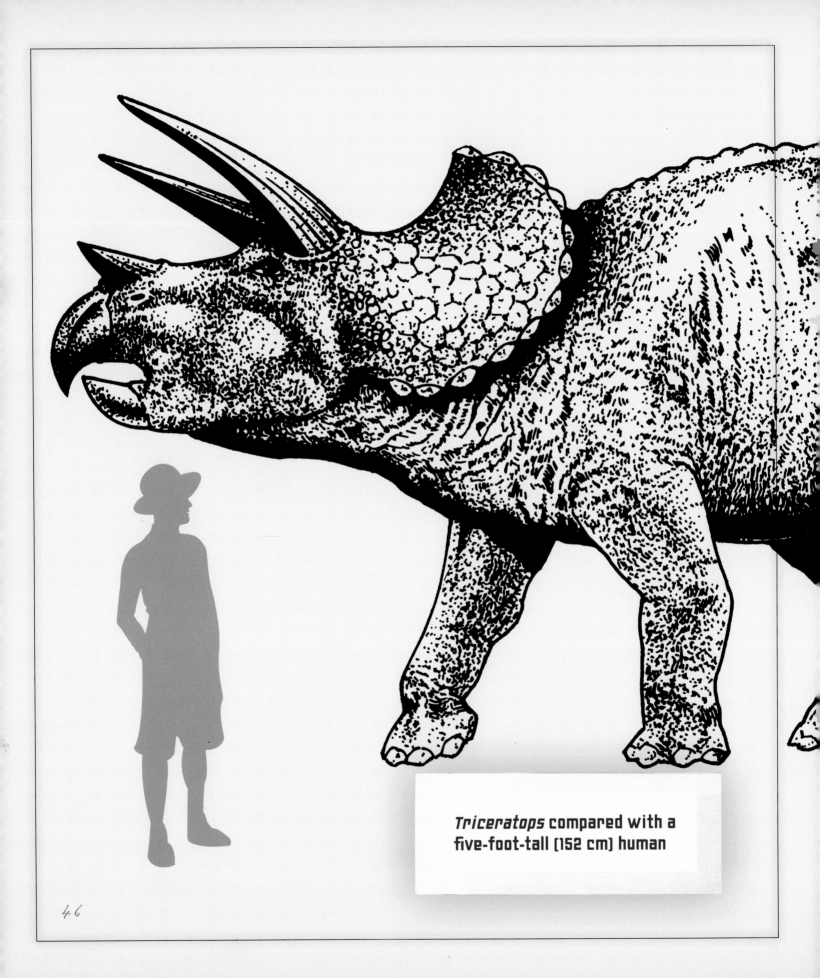

Triceratops compared with a five-foot-tall [152 cm] human

GLOSSARY

carnivores—animals that feed on other animals

climates—the long-term weather conditions of areas

conifers—evergreen trees, such as pines and firs, that bear cones

curator—the person in charge of a museum or art collection

cycads—tropical palmlike plants that bear large cones

evolving—adapting or changing over time to survive in a certain environment

extinction—the act or process of becoming extinct; coming to an end or dying out

ginkgoes—large, ornamental trees with fan-shaped leaves, fleshy fruit, and edible nuts

herbivores—animals that feed only on plants

horn core—the fossilized, innermost section of an animal's horn; it is usually only a fraction of the size it would have been when the animal was alive

mammals—warm-blooded animals that have a backbone and hair or fur, give birth to live young, and produce milk to feed their young

migrated—traveled from one region or climate to another for feeding or breeding purposes

paleontologist—a scientist who studies fossilized plants and animals

reptiles—cold-blooded animals with scaly skin that typically lay eggs on land

scavengers—animals that eat the rotting flesh of animals found dead

sediment—crushed, rocky matter that settles to the bottom of a liquid, such as a body of water

species—a group of living organisms that share similar characteristics and can mate with one another

status symbol—a possession or feature regarded as a mark of high social standing

vertebrae—the series of small bones forming the backbone

SELECTED BIBLIOGRAPHY

Barrett, Paul. *National Geographic Dinosaurs*. Washington, D.C.: National Geographic Society, 2001.

Burnie, David. *The Kingfisher Illustrated Dinosaur Encyclopedia*. New York: Kingfisher Publications, 2001.

Colbert, Edwin H. *The Great Dinosaur Hunters and Their Discoveries*. New York: Dover Publications, 1984.

Farlow, James O., and M. K. Brett-Surman. *The Complete Dinosaur*. Bloomington, Ind.: Indiana University Press, 1997.

Kimmel, Elizabeth Cody. *Dinosaur Bone War: Cope and Marsh's Fossil Feud*. New York: Random House Books for Young Readers, 2006.

Parker, Steve. *Dinosaurus: The Complete Guide to Dinosaurs*. Buffalo, N.Y.: Firefly Books, 2003.

INDEX

READ MORE

Due, Andrea. *Dinosaur Profile: Triceratops*. Farmington Hills, Mich.: Blackbirch Press, 2004.

Lansky, Kathryn. *Dinosaur Dig*. New York: Morrow Junior Books, 1990.

Matthews, Rupert. *Dinosaur Dictionary*. New York: Tangerine Press, 2001.

Ottaviani, Jim. *Bone Sharps, Cowboys, and Thunder Lizards*. Ann Arbor, Mich.: G-T Labs, 2005.

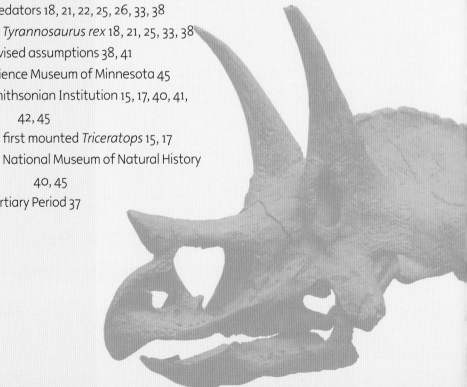